Weevil K. Neevil: Stuntbug

by

Colin Dowland

Illustrated by Peter Firmin

You do not need to read this page -
just get on with the book!

First published in Great Britain by Barrington Stoke Ltd
10 Belford Terrace, Edinburgh EH4 3DQ
Copyright © 2001 Colin Dowland
Illustrations © Peter Firmin
The moral right of the author has been asserted in
accordance with the Copyright, Designs and
Patents Act 1988
ISBN 1-902260-84-8
Printed by Polestar AUP Aberdeen Ltd
Reprinted 2002

MEET THE AUTHOR – COLIN DOWLAND

What is your favourite animal?
The armadillo
What is your favourite boy's name?
Anything but Colin!
What is your favourite girl's name?
Her name is Ann
What is your favourite food?
Smelly cheese
What is your favourite music?
Jazz, classical or corny
What is your favourite hobby?
D.I.Y.

MEET THE ILLUSTRATOR – PETER FIRMIN

What is your favourite animal?
My Jack Russell dog, Bobbie
What is your favourite boy's name?
Charlie, my Dad's name.
What is your favourite girl's name?
My wife's name, Joan.
What is your favourite food?
Sprats and cockles
What is your favourite music?
We've always had dogs,
so I have to say Bach!
What is your favourite hobby?
Making things – especially toys

For beautiful Martha
A book you can chew
Your Grandad liked this one
I hope you do too

Contents

Chapter 1
Crash Landing

The kitchen cupboard was dark. The lids were tight upon the jam jars and the cornflake box was sealed up for the night. Not a munch or a crunch could be heard. In the kitchen drawers not a single spoon stirred.

The kitchen clock struck midnight.

Weevil K. Neevil woke with a jolt. He was lying on the Bottom Shelf of the cupboard with only blackness all around him. For a moment he thought he was dead. He stretched out his feelers and checked his shell with two of his six feet. There were no cracks. Not even a scratch or a dent. It couldn't be true. He had survived the horrific fall. He was alive!

Standing up onto all six feet, he felt something soft beneath him. One nibble told him what a lucky beetle he had been. His parents had always warned him that too much sugar was bad for his health. But it had just saved his life. He had landed right in the middle of the sugar bowl.

Mr and Mrs Neevil, his parents, had raised 26 little grubs altogether. Like most weevils, his parents had very poor memories. They had named each baby grub after a letter of the alphabet to make it easier to remember. Weevil was number eleven and so he had been called Weevil *K.* Neevil.

He was big for his age and much more curious than his brothers and sisters. He had always wanted more from his life than just eating crumbs from sunrise to sunset. Weevil K. Neevil wanted the whole cream cracker, the full chocolate biscuit. He knew that there were exciting adventures waiting for him. He would not find them among the heavy bags of flour and rice on the Top Shelf. He wanted to explore the big, wide kitchen out there.

He had tried to tell his father about his dreams.

His father would simply reply, "Just eat up your grub, Grub," and would carry on munching his crumbs.

Weevil's fall had been his own stupid fault. Up on the Top Shelf, he and his brothers had been playing rugby with a grain of rice. It was getting dark and his parents had called them in for supper. He knew it would be crackers for supper yet again and he was bored with them.

Weevil took no notice of his parents' calls. He kicked the ball high into the air

and chased after it as fast as his tiny legs could go. In the dim light, he had not seen the edge of the Top Shelf coming towards him. He ran on without thinking and before he knew it, he had stepped out into dark, empty space.

With a weevily scream, he fell. His legs grabbed wildly at the air. Down and down and down he went, landing in the bowl of sugar with a soft thud.

Weevil now began the steep climb up the handle of the sugar spoon. He knew he was about to start one of those exciting adventures that he had always dreamed about. He also knew that his worried parents were way up above him on the Top Shelf, amongst the flour and the biscuits. He did not know if he would ever see them again.

He dropped lightly off the end of the
sugar spoon and into the strange world of
the Bottom Shelf.

What he saw in front of him would
change his life forever.

Chapter 2
Lucky Break

It was unlike anything he had seen before. Squeezed in between the bottles and jars was a large upturned coffee filter held in position by tight ropes of straining spaghetti. It was like an enormous tent. Written on one side in big, bold letters were the words: 'GERRY BLUEBOTTLE'S CIRCUS.'

It took Weevil's breath away. His feelers twitched in amazement. He scuttled forwards towards a gap in the tent that looked like a door.

He pushed his head inside and gasped.

The tent was buzzing with insects. Each one was busy practising a special circus routine.

A daddy-longlegs on stilts, dressed as a clown, pushed past Weevil into the centre of a huge ring. A large cockroach was juggling six clubs at once. A small group of fireflies were spitting flames at each other and a Chinese dragonfly in a glittering costume was trying out an exotic dance.

Nearby, a group of flea acrobats were being ticked off by their trainer. At the far end of the circus ring, a silverfish dived from a high ladder and splashed noisily into a small diving pool below. High above

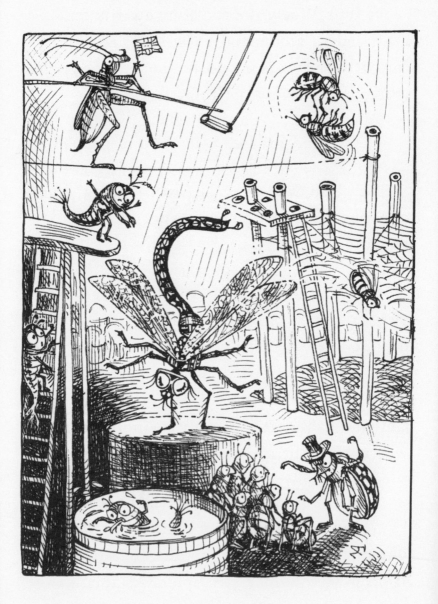

it all, flying ants threw themselves from one trapeze to another. They linked wings and legs and performed hair-raising twists and turns over a safety net made of a spider's web.

As he gazed into the tent, Weevil knew that this was what he had been looking for. This was better than crummy crumbs or boring biscuits. This was life in the fast lane. This was the life for Weevil K. Neevil.

"The show ain't until later, pal," boomed a voice behind him.

Weevil jumped. Turning round, he was met by a large thick-necked bluebottle fly. He wore a big suit, a big hat and sucked on a big, fat cigar.

"You have to pay like the rest of the crowd," continued the fly, waving the cigar at Weevil.

Weevil thought quickly. He had a cracker-crunchingly, brilliant idea.

"I've not come to see the show," Weevil replied, "I've come to see Gerry Bluebottle himself."

The fly blew a cloud of cigar smoke into the air. "You're looking right at him, pal. What can I do for you?"

"You see, Mr Bluebottle," Weevil stuttered, "I'm ... I'm ... looking for a job."

Gerry Bluebottle rubbed his front legs together and twitched his wings. "You know, pal," he grinned with a twinkle in one of his eyes, "You're in luck."

Chapter 3
Great Balls Of Dung!

Cleaning up after the Dazzling Dung Beetles wasn't exactly what Weevil had had in mind. It was amazing to see them balancing on top of their balls of dung. But shovelling all that mess away after the show was probably the second worst job at the circus. The worst job was cleaning out the horsefly stables. Weevil had to do that too.

Still, it was a start. He had joined the circus and life was indeed more exciting than on the Top Shelf amongst the biscuits. In return for his work, he was given food and a safe place to stay the night.

Sleeping in the stables with the horseflies wasn't exactly what he had expected either, but this was the circus.

For the next few nights, Weevil watched the show spellbound. It was the most exciting thing that he had ever seen.

The jugglers never dropped a ball. The flying ants leapt from trapeze to trapeze with perfect timing. The flea acrobats tumbled and rolled and jumped in a superb display.

Bees balanced plates on their stings. The horseflies shook their feather plumes as they did their tricks around the ring.

In between the acts, the daddy-longlegs
clowns tottered about on their stilts,
throwing water and chasing each other out
of the tent.

The only thing that disappointed Weevil was the crowd. Hardly anybody came to watch the show. The tent was almost empty.

A caterpillar sat on one side of the ring, taking up six seats. On the other side were a small family of woodlice and two old ladybirds in large hats. A scattering of

mites and midges around the ring made up the rest of the crowd. Everywhere else there were just rows and rows of empty seats.

At the end of the show, Gerry Bluebottle called everyone into his office. He was counting out the tickets that had been sold that afternoon. "Fourteen, fifteen, sixteen, seventeen. That's it, folks," he sighed. "I just can't afford to keep running this show if no-one comes to see it. And if no-one comes to see it, there ain't no wages."

"And if there ain't no wages," chipped in an old flea, "there ain't no acts."

"The insects in this place just don't want to see the same old acts no more," continued Gerry Bluebottle, shrugging his wings.

A great buzz of insect chatter broke out among the performers. The horseflies' trainer started talking about setting up a riding school. The plate-spinning bees buzzed angrily that they would have to go back to making honey.

Gerry Bluebottle twitched his wings and stood up. "I'll give it to the end of the week. Tonight, tomorrow and the next day. If it ain't picked up by then, then the show's over, folks. I'll just have to close the circus down."

Chapter 4
Mind Blowing

For a few wonderful days Weevil had never felt so happy. Now it looked as if the circus would close down. As the acts got ready for the evening performance and Weevil returned to the stables, he had never felt worse. For the first time in his life, he had found something he really wanted to do. In a few short days his dream could all be over.

"Earwigs' droppings and wasps' teeth," he cursed, booting the side of a large cornflake box with his third foot. The box was almost empty. It toppled over, nearly crushing him. The last few broken flakes spilt out onto the shelf.

Weevil scuttled over to the flakes. He half tidied the mess and half nibbled at the pieces. At first, he did not take any notice of the shiny corner of a plastic bag that was sticking up out of the last few flakes.

Then, as he tried to push the plastic bag back inside the box, he noticed something gleaming silver and red inside it. He brushed away the bits of cornflakes. It was a strange thing to have in a box of cereal.

Weevil dragged the bag back out of the box and began tearing at the plastic with four of his feet. He ripped and pulled and

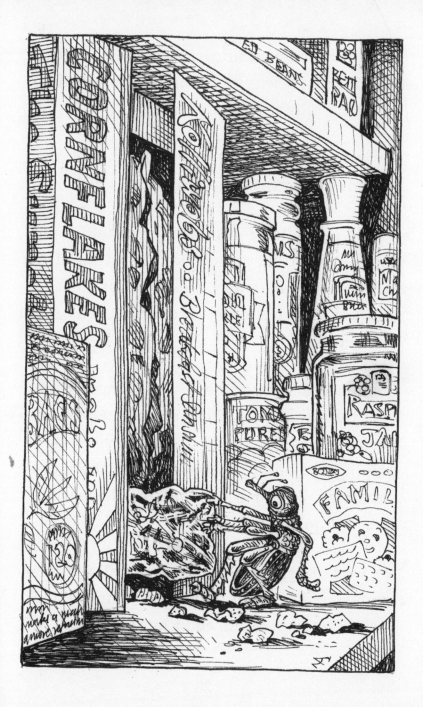

pulled and ripped until he could see what it was inside. It was the most amazing silver and red, shiny, new motorbike.

"Wow!" he gasped, running his feelers lovingly over the gleaming paintwork.

He struggled for several minutes to put the bike onto its stand. He needed all of his strength to lift it up at all. He stood back and admired his new discovery. It was mind blowing.

In the distance, Weevil could hear the entrance music for the start of the evening performance. He really should have been helping the dung beetles get into their costumes. But such an amazing discovery was too good to miss.

Weevil brushed away the cornflake dust from the chain and engine and sat astride the monster bike. Already he felt like a racing champion. He tried the brakes and turned the throttle. It looked real enough, but he didn't think for one minute that it would actually start.

Carefully he placed his third foot onto the kickstart pedal. He steadied himself, then jumped high into the air, landing with all his tiny weight onto the pedal.

Chapter 5
Out Of Control

The motorbike roared into life underneath him and sped off at high speed. Weevil hung on for dear life. Knowing nothing about the controls, he tried to steer as best he could. He zoomed in between jam jars, teabags and old bottles of vinegar. He charged over a bar of chocolate, his shell shaking at every lumpy chunk.

Across the shelf he zoomed, totally out of control now. He was heading in one direction – straight towards the circus tent.

There was nothing Weevil could do. The handlebars seemed to be locked in one position. He was still picking up speed and the tent was getting closer.

He shut his eyes and hung on until, with a huge 'RRRRIIIIPPP', he tore a hole in the side of the tent and sped off into the centre of the ring.

The dung beetles were about to finish their act and Weevil was heading straight towards one of their balls of dung. He gave a last tug at the handlebars which suddenly loosened. He turned to one side just in time.

Round and round the ring Weevil went, getting dizzier and dizzier. He twisted the handlebars again and took a path across the ring. He knocked a daddy-longlegs off its stilts along the way.

Up in between the half-empty seats he rode, trailing the spider's web safety net behind him. He picked up a young ladybird selling programmes onto the front of the handlebars as it zoomed along.

With another sharp twist, he raced back down the middle of the tent. He was heading straight towards the pool where the high-diving silverfish landed.

He tried to turn again, but the extra weight of the programme seller up front made it impossible. She screamed and her programmes flew into his face. He couldn't see where he was going.

Then, with an enormous thud that shook the tent, he hit the edge of the diving pool.

Weevil and the programme seller were sent
flying over the handlebars and landed with a
huge splash in the diving pool.

Chapter 6
Think You're Clever?

After the show was over, Weevil limped his way from the horsefly stables towards Gerry Bluebottle's office.

He had been dripping wet from feeler to toe and had to dry himself off with the corner of a teabag. He was a bit battered and shaken and he'd twisted two of his legs.

But what was really worrying him was the thought that he was in big trouble. Gerry Bluebottle wanted to see him in his office – right now.

Weevil took a deep breath and knocked feebly at the door of Gerry Bluebottle's office.

"Come in," said the gruff voice.

Blushing all over his shell, Weevil opened the door and went in.

Gerry Bluebottle sat in his swivel chair with his back to the door, reading a fly-paper. A cloud of cigar smoke hung above him.

The swivel chair spun round quickly and Weevil took a step back.

"Sit yourself down, young Weevil," he ordered, folding up his paper and putting it on the desk.

Weevil did as he was told.

Gerry Bluebottle sucked thoughtfully on his cigar. "I suppose you thought it was mighty clever busting into the big top and making such a scene like that an' all?" he hissed.

Weevil shook his head.

"And I suppose that you thought it was clever hijacking one of my young programme sellers too?" he continued. He jabbed his cigar towards Weevil and spilled ash onto the shelf.

Weevil's face went scarlet and tears formed behind his tiny eyes.

"And I suppose you thought that making a big splash at the end was a mighty clever thing to do, did you?"

Weevil gulped. "No ... Mr Bluebottle ... Sir ... I'm ..."

Gerry Bluebottle stood up sharply and stubbed out his cigar. "Well ... " he bellowed, "I sure do!!!" and he roared with laughter. "What you did tonight was the best thing that's happened to this circus for years and years. The crowd are still talking about it now – said it was the best thing they'd ever seen."

Weevil was confused. What was Gerry Bluebottle saying? It must be the cigar smoke affecting his tiny brain.

"Now the big question is," said Gerry Bluebottle, putting a wing around Weevil's shoulders, "can you do it all again for the show tomorrow?"

Chapter 7
As Dry As A Cracker

That night, Weevil hardly slept at all. He was so excited. This was his big chance to make a name for himself.

The next morning he got up at dawn and crept quietly out of the horsefly stables. His motorbike had survived the crash well. It only had a few minor scratches to the paintwork. It was the diving pool that had come out of it badly. A

couple of woodlice had been made to stay
up all night patching up the leaks.

After a quick check, Weevil soon realised
why his motorbike had spun out of control.
The throttle had been stuck in the full-on
position by a tiny piece of cornflake.

He solved the problem by simply eating
it. Then he put some olive oil onto the
handlebars to loosen them up and as quick
as a flea he was ready to get back onto his
dream machine.

He lifted three legs carefully over the saddle and sat down. It felt good, but he was a little scared. He took a deep breath and flicked out the kickstart pedal. Then he jumped high into the air and landed feet first onto the pedal. Nothing happened. He tried again, jumping even higher, but again nothing happened. The engine was dead.

Weevil panicked and began jumping up and down again and again like a crazy grasshopper. Finally, worn out, he slumped forward. He wondered if his chance at the big time was over.

"Perhaps you need some fuel," said a soft voice behind him.

Weevil jumped.

There, sitting on the spoon of the sugar bowl, was the young ladybird programme seller who Weevil had picked up on the handlebars the night before.

Weevil's feelers blushed.

"Everyone calls me Dotty," she said, jumping down from the sugar bowl and holding out her first hand for Weevil to shake. "I'm training to be the first ever tightrope-walking ladybird."

Weevil shook her hand, cleared his throat and shuffled his feet shyly. "I didn't have a chance to say sorry yesterday for ..."

"... giving me a lift," added Dotty with an understanding smile.

Weevil nodded.

"I was all right once I'd dried off," she continued. "Although my backside is a bit sore. I suppose it was quite exciting really."

There was a brief silence.

"So *have* you got any fuel in the tank

then?" she asked, pointing towards the motorbike.

Weevil undid the cap to the fuel tank and peered inside.

"It's as dry as a cracker," he said gloomily. His voice echoed into the hole. "Now I'll never get my big chance."

"You're not much of a fighter, are you?" said Dotty. "I know where there is plenty of fuel."

"Where?" asked Weevil, not believing a word of it.

Dotty pointed. "Right behind you on the shelf."

Weevil turned round. Behind him was a small bottle of cooking brandy. "You're a genius, Dotty," cried Weevil, running off towards the horsefly stables.

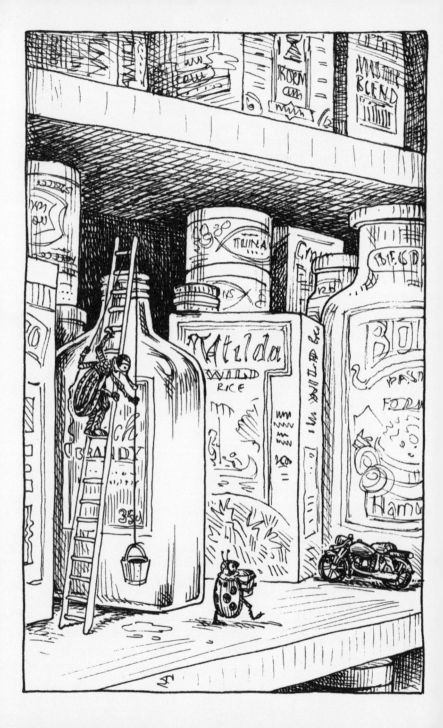

Chapter 8
Burning Rubber

Weevil fetched a rope, some buckets and a ladder from the stables. Using these, he and Dotty collected enough brandy in the buckets to last for days. The motorbike tank was full to the brim with brandy fuel and Weevil was all ready to go.

He climbed back onto the saddle with much more confidence, turned the throttle to zero, gave a huge jump and slammed onto the kickstart pedal. This time the motorbike roared into life underneath him.

The noise was deafening. It was still early and Weevil was sure to have woken anyone who was still in bed. He gave the thumbs up to Dotty and slowly turned the throttle. Off he went.

First he practised riding in straight lines to get used to the feel of the heavy bike. Then came turns, big circles, starts and stops.

As he became more confident, Weevil began to lift the front wheel off the ground, hopping on just the back wheel. Next came slides and controlled skids. The smell of burning rubber drifted through the cupboard shelves.

At lunchtime, Weevil was seen talking excitedly with a team of woodlice. The woodlice listened, nodded and then scurried off to hammer together some props for Weevil's act that night. One of the flea acrobats lent Weevil a costume. It itched a bit, but at least it had six legs.

Dotty added some sparkly tassels that would flap in the wind as Weevil rode along.

As the day went by, Weevil became more and more confident. Backwards and forwards he raced along the shelf on his bike. He tried out different speeds and experimented with ramps and hoops. A small crowd of young bugs gathered around to watch him practise his tricks.

Weevil and his motorbike were as difficult to part as a wasp and a picnic. He was a gifted, natural bike rider. He and his machine were as one. By the end of the day, when the circus lights came on for the evening show, Weevil had his complete routine ready to perform.

Chapter 9
Packed To Burstin'

A few minutes before the show, Weevil took a look into the tent. It was full to the brim with insects from all over the shelves. Gerry Bluebottle hadn't lost any time spreading the word. Weevil's name was lit up in a bright, new sign outside the tent. It had attracted moths and midges for miles around.

There was a buzz of excitement around the ring, especially from the bees and wasps.

Weevil left the tent and began putting on his costume and polishing his motorbike. He was getting nervous.

Gerry Bluebottle burst into his dressing room, carrying a huge handful of cash and a big smile on his face. Ticket sales had never been better. "It's packed to burstin' out there tonight. I've put you on last as a grand finale," he grinned. "We need a big finish and I'm countin' on you, kid."

He thumped Weevil heavily on the back and went off to count his money.

It was almost too much to bear. He was to perform after the flying ants, but first he would have to sit nervously through all the other acts.

"I brought you this," chirped a voice that jolted Weevil from his nervous daydream. It was Dotty holding a battered piece of metal. "It's a horsefly shoe," she continued. "For good luck."

Dotty turned a little redder than usual, then flew off before Weevil could even say thanks.

Weevil took the shoe and tucked it inside his costume. He had begun to feel better already.

At last the music started and the show began. Weevil watched as the other performers did their acts. It would soon be his turn.

As the clapping for the flying ants died away, there was a roll on the drums. Gerry Bluebottle stepped into the ring and began his introduction.

"Larvaes and Gentlebugs," he boomed.
"Now for the moment you have all been
waiting for. The latest sensation from
Gerry Bluebottle's world famous circus.
Please put your wings together and give a
big welcome to the amazing ... the

astonishing ... the death-defying ... the daredevil skill ... of ...

WEEVIL ... *K.* ... NEEVIL."

Chapter 10
Stuntbug Showtime

Outside the tent, Weevil roared the motorbike into life. He let off the brake and sped into the ring. His feelers flew back in the wind and the sparkly tassels of his jacket flapped wildly. He headed through the centre of the ring, straight for the diving pool.

This time, however, he was in full control. He turned at the last minute, kicking up a cloud of dust from the circus floor. Then, with amazing ease, he tugged on the handlebars and did a wheelie all the way back along the way he had come in. There was a gasp from the audience and a thunder of applause.

He skidded to a halt. Weevil waited. He pumped the throttle, impatient to go. The team of woodlice dragged two large hoops into the centre of the ring. A firefly came forward and lit the hoops which smoked and sizzled with tall, yellow flames. One lollystick ramp was set up in front of the hoops and one behind them. Weevil revved his engine.

He was ready for *The Onion Rings of Fire*.

There was a roll on the drums and Weevil hit the throttle. Faster and faster he raced towards the lollysticks. He hit them

perfectly and soared up into the air through first one flaming ring, then the next, landing safely on the second lollystick ramp. The audience went wild. There was no stopping Weevil now.

Next it was the tricks. Up on the saddle he stood, only two of his feet in contact with the bike. In and out of some sugar lumps he darted. He did it first forwards, then facing backwards and then standing on the handlebars. He even did it blindfolded.

At last it was time for the biggest stunt of all. Once again the woodlice set up their equipment. A cranefly was brought in to lift some huge boxes into the centre of the ring.

Weevil waited calmly now. He must concentrate his mind fully on his most difficult trick. The lollystick ramps were set up again but this time they were pointed skywards. Weevil rode slowly towards the first ramp to practise the angle for take-off.

A ripple of excitement ran through the crowd. Weevil would now attempt his most difficult stunt.

When everything was ready, Weevil gave the thumbs up. Gerry Bluebottle stepped once more into the centre of the ring.

"Your attention, please," he boomed, waiting for the crowd to settle. "Weevil K. Neevil will now attempt a stunt so dangerous that it has never been attempted by any other performer in the insect world. Weevil K. Neevil will jump seven boxes of matches ... in one leap."

There was a gasp from the crowd.

Gerry Bluebottle twitched his wings. "I must ask for complete silence."

The lights dimmed. It was dark except for a single spotlight that focused on Weevil. The crowd grew silent. Then more spotlights lit up the huge boxes in front of him.

Weevil looked straight ahead. He revved his engine and his back wheel spun. He released the brakes and sprang forward at terrific speed. Faster and faster he went, zooming towards the first ramp. He hit it perfectly. High into the air he soared passing one, two, three boxes. Four, five and six flew by.

As he approached the final box, something was wrong. He was losing balance. The motorbike twisted to one side. He was out of control.

With a sickening thud, the motorbike scraped onto the far ramp. Weevil struggled to regain control, but skidded off the side of the lollystick. He was thrown from the saddle and tumbled over and over crashing headfirst into a ball of dung.

The crowd went silent. Gerry Bluebottle and the other performers ran towards Weevil, who lay quite still.

Gerry Bluebottle took off his hat and knelt down by the side of Weevil's twisted body. He shook his head.

Dotty began to sniffle and the performers bowed their heads. In the crowd, parents took their crying children under their wings.

For a moment no-one spoke. There was deathly silence.

Chapter 11
Smelly Superstar

"This stuff stinks," said a muffled weevily voice from inside the ball of dung. "Get it off me!"

Gerry Bluebottle leapt to his feet. "He's alive!" he shouted. "It's a pesky miracle."

With a little help from Dotty, Weevil's head was pulled from the ball of dung. He struggled to sit up and then stood groggily on his feet.

"You'd better wave to your fans, young Weevil," Gerry Bluebottle urged him, rubbing his legs together and dreaming of what he could do with his new superstar stuntbug.

Weevil held up a leg, ignoring the pain and waved to the crowd. Dotty lent over to kiss him, smelt the dung and changed her mind. The crowd stood up, stamping their many feet, clapping their wings together and cheering wildly.

The flea acrobats lifted Weevil onto their shoulders and carried him around the ring. Cheering rang out from every corner of the tent.

Weevil was a hero ... a superstar ... a cracker-crushing, biscuit-bashing stuntbug.

Chapter 12
Unexpected Fans

After the show was over, Weevil found himself surrounded by young bugs wanting his autograph. They were desperate to meet the new superstar and to have their circus programmes signed.

Dotty had bandaged his head with a scrap of kitchen roll. She now stood protectively next to him, trying to keep him from getting crushed by his fans.

Weevil was dazed by his new-found
fame. He stood there with one leg in a sling
and three pens busy scribbling autographs.

He was so busy signing programmes
that he failed to notice a couple of not quite
so young weevils hanging back behind his
younger fans.

"Can we have your autograph, too, Mr K. Neevil?" croaked one of them over the top of the younger bugs' heads.

"Just for our 26 children," added the other.

"Sure," said Weevil, looking up for a moment.

Weevily eyes met weevily eyes. Feelers sensed a familiar face. It was a moment that Weevil would never forget. A moment of bug-stunning surprise.

"Hello, son," said the old pair together, smiling broadly.

Weevil dropped his pens. He couldn't speak.

It was his parents.

"We didn't know you were a superstar," choked his Mum. She wiped away proud tears with the corner of a napkin.

"And we didn't know you had a girlfriend," grinned his Dad, nudging Weevil in the ribs and pointing to Dotty.

Weevil went bright red. He thought he must be dreaming. The crash must have done something to his head. But before he had a chance to work it out, his parents crushed him in a hug of many weevil legs. It felt better than jumping any amount of matchboxes.

"But I'll tell you one thing," said his Dad, turning to the beaming Dotty. "We've always known he was crackers!!"

Weevil K. Neevil could only manage a single word. "Crrrrumbs."

Bye.bye!

Who is Barrington Stoke?

Barrington Stoke was a famous and much-loved story-teller. He travelled from village to village carrying a lantern to light his way. He arrived as it grew dark and when the young boys and girls of the village saw the glow of his lantern, they hurried to the central meeting place. They were full of excitement and expectation, for his stories were always wonderful.

Then Barrington Stoke set down his lantern. In the flickering light the listeners were enthralled by his tales of adventure, horror and mystery. He knew exactly what they liked best and he loved telling a good story. And another. And then another. When the lantern burned low and dawn was nearly breaking, he slipped away. He was gone by morning, only to appear the next day in some other village to tell the next story.

Barrington Stoke would like to thank all its readers for commenting on the manuscript before publication and in particular:

Sam Anderson
Deirdre Vaughan Brown
Judy Cochand
Hannah Evans
James Evans
Robert Ferguson
Harry Fitz-Gerald
Josh Gajree
Thomas Gillingham
Sam Hayes
Jacqui Horsburgh
Daniel Jackson

Frances Johnston
Anna King
Fiona Lewis
Albert Martin
Chi Chi McFarlane
Robert Miller
David Moffat
Natasha Moncrieff
Ian Reid
James Salisbury
Charlotte Wilson
Annabel Yarrow

Become a Consultant!

Would you like to give us feedback on our titles before they are published? Contact us at the address or website below - we'd love to hear from you!

Barrington Stoke, 10 Belford Terrace, Edinburgh EH4 3DQ
Tel: 0131 315 4933 Fax: 0131 315 4934
E-mail: info@barringtonstoke.demon.co.uk
Website: www.barringtonstoke.co.uk

If you loved this story, why don't you read . . .

Billy the Squid

by Colin Dowland

Do you like adventure stories? This one takes place under the sea.
Something very fishy is going on down there. Can anyone save the town from the claws of a monster? If you have a wacky sense of humour, dive into this book!

Visit our website!
www.barrringtonstoke.co.uk